Calm Down, COOPER!

For Isaac & Zachariah – LM

To my family, for always being behind me – AC

Edited by Helen Brown
& Hannah Daffern
Designed by Jack Clucas
Cover design by John Bigwood

First published in Great Britain in 2020 by Buster Books,
an imprint of Michael O'Mara Books Limited,
9 Lion Yard, Tremadoc Road, London SW4 7NQ

W www.mombooks.com/buster   f Buster Books   🐦 @BusterBooks

ISBN: 978-1-78055-570-6

2 4 6 8 10 9 7 5 3 1

This book was printed in March 2020 by Leo Paper Products Ltd,
Heshan Astros Printing Limited, Xuantan Temple Industrial Zone,
Gulao Town, Heshan City, Guangdong Province, China.

Calm Down, COOPER!

Written by Lily Murray

Illustrated by Anna Chernyshova

Buster Books

Cooper was the perfect pup,
The happiest pooch in town.

He loved his owner, Martha,
And he never let her down.

He fetched her slippers in the morning ...

... wiped his paws upon the mat.

He kept the house in order ...

... and never chased the cat.

"Cooper, aren't you wonderful,"
Martha loved to say.
"I know that I can trust you,
In each and every way."

But could it last forever?
For there came a fateful day
when Martha's Great Aunt Mildred
came to the house to stay.

"Just look who I've brought with me,"
She said, pulling off a scarf.
"It's my darling parrot, Pandy.
Oh, how he makes me laugh."

PANDEMONIUM

"He came from Timbuktu, you know,
He's really very clever.
I think you'll find he's good as gold,
No trouble whatsoever."

Then Martha turned to Cooper,
"We're off out for the day.
We'll be back at half past nine,
You're in charge while I'm away."

Cooper nodded proudly.
This was his chance to shine.
But as soon as they had left the house,
Pandy squawked ...

"IT'S PARTY TIME!"

"I've invited my friends over,
I've told them your address.
I hope that you're excited,
I've said it's fancy dress."

Cooper felt a clutch of fear,
"What will our owners say?"
"Calm down, Cooper!" said Pandy.
"Let's have fun while they're away."

The doorbell started ringing,
And a lion walked through the door.
He was wearing silk pyjamas,
With a tuba in his paw.

He was followed by a rhino,
And a gang of wildebeest.
They brought along a yummy cake
and yelled, "It's time to feast!"

Next came a troupe

of penguins,

Who

tap

danced

down

the

stairs.

And a gorilla called Camilla,

Juggling apricots and pears.

Cooper dashed among them,
Trying to calm the party down,
Then in waltzed an ostrich
in the most amazing gown.

There was a panther in the pantry,
And ten snakes in the sink,
A dance-off in the kitchen,
And a zebra dressed in pink.

"Don't break the plates!" begged Cooper.
"No sliding down the stairs.
And really, Mr Hippo,
You're too heavy for those chairs."

"Pandy, this is terrible.
Oh, can't you make it stop?
I'm trying to tidy up here,
But a meerkat's got my mop."

But Pandy was too busy
with a laughing cockatoo.
They started singing loudly,
"Calm down, Cooper! Join in, too."

"You must go now," pleaded Cooper.
"It's nearly half past nine.
Our owners will be back soon,
We're running out of time!"

"We'll be fine," said Pandy.
But then a key turned in the lock.
It was Martha and Aunt Mildred.
Poor Cooper froze in shock.

"There's only one thing for it,"
Pandy whispered round the house.
"Turn off the lights and hide.
Be as quiet as a mouse."

Just a moment later,
The front door opened wide.
Martha and Aunt Mildred
came bustling inside.

"Oh, my darling Cooper.
What a lovely sight.
I knew I could rely on you.
I'll just turn on this light ... "

Martha's mouth fell open.
"My house is such a mess!
There's an elephant in my fireplace,
And a gorilla in my dress."

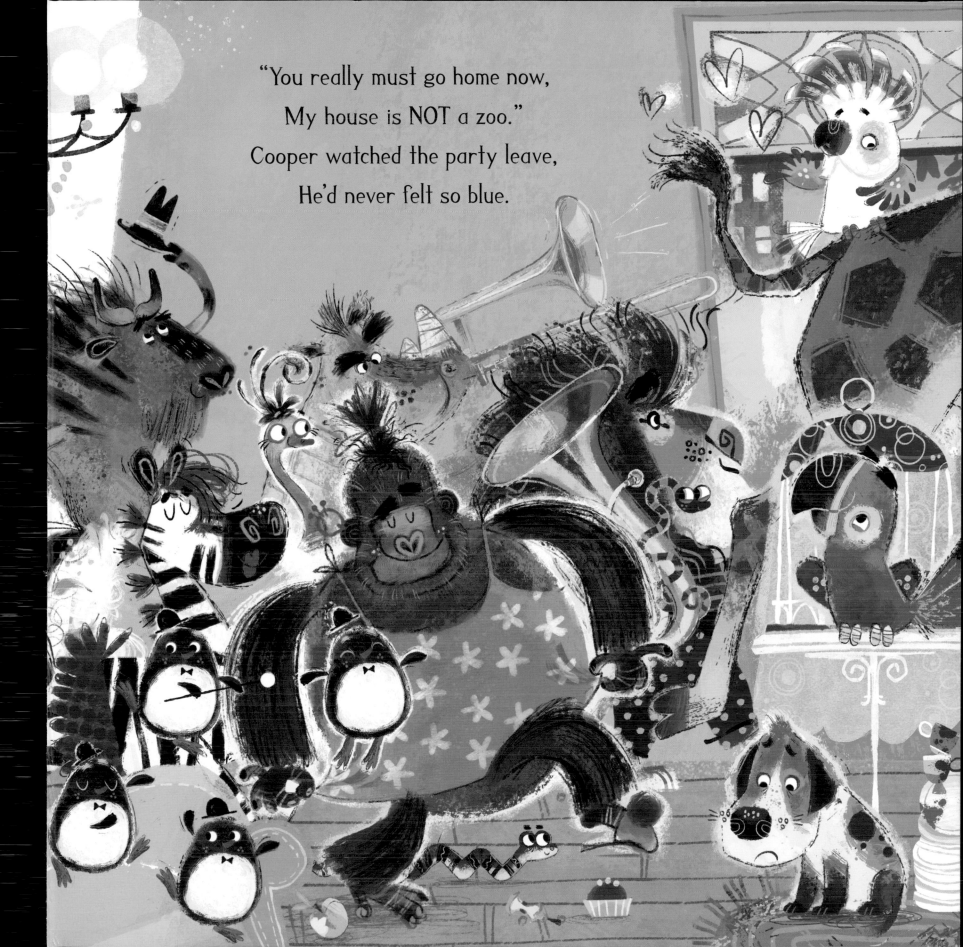

"You really must go home now,
My house is NOT a zoo."
Cooper watched the party leave,
He'd never felt so blue.

"Don't worry, Cooper," said Martha.
"Things don't always go to plan.
Despite the mess, you tried your best,
And I'm still your biggest fan."